W9-BCU-298

Shoot for the moon ...
Even if you miss, you'll
still be among the stars ...

Karin Tillisch is a well-known horse journalist who works with the
Shadow Show Team. Born March 10, 1978 in the small German village
of Sasbachwalden where she still lives with her two horses, Shadow and
Starlight, Karin started riding at the age of three. She has written two previous
horse books – one about gaited horses and one about trick horse training.

Original title: Shadow - das Pferd, das aus dem Schatten kam
© Stabenfeldt 2005
Photos: Karin Tillisch, Sita Stepper, Roland Erdrich, Marianne Tillisch,
Solke Teuber, Katja Schäfer, Ingo Ehrmeier
Layout: Kristin Eriksen Berg
Translator: Karen Nickel Anhalt
Editor: Bobbie Chase
Printed in Italy 2005

ISBN:1-933343-17-6

Shadow

– the horse that emerged from the shadows

By Karin Tillisch
Translated by Karen Nickel Anhalt

Shadow – a few words about an extraordinary horse

It isn't easy to describe Shadow. He has such a complex, dazzling personality that it's hard to know where to start!

What really makes him special, though, is how he makes people laugh – how he can conjure up a sparkle in their eyes. Whether at a tournament, a big show or just at home in the stable, people can't just walk past him without stopping. There's something about him – he attracts young and old like a magnet.

He makes people smile, because they can truly feel this horse's vitality and energy. With his little tricks, Shadow amazes them. And makes them think.

There's nothing he wouldn't do for me

"Sometimes I have the feeling that Shadow loves you so much that he wants to surpass even himself to do things for you that he isn't able to do yet," said Sita Stepper, the World Open champion in the Western riding discipline, Superhorse. "A good horse always does his best. But Shadow does more than his best – he puts his whole heart and soul into it."

Many horses have had an influence on my life. First and foremost, there was Tanya, the Shetland pony that carried me around quietly and patiently when I was three years old. And then there were those disturbing school horses at the local riding club, where I spent more time under my horse than I did in the saddle. They didn't teach me anything positive, but they did influence the way I think about horses today. Never again will I go to a riding stable where the school horses are seen as nothing more than a way to make money and are forced to spend their entire lives in dark, dank riding stables! After the riding club fiasco came Excalibur's Mystery, the Tennessee Walker colt that gave me the courage to get back in the saddle again after a serious accident. Next came Marfio, the Hanoverian gelding, who slowly made my fears disappear completely. And finally, there was Kiera, the Wuerttemberger mare. Through her I learned to communicate with horses the way they do and to truly understand them.

But Shadow had the greatest influence of all on me.

"Karen would not be Karen if it weren't for Shadow," said Marcus, our feed dealer, who knew Shadow long before I did.

That pretty much sums it up, really. Shadow changed my life completely. He helped me to forget my fear of horses, as well as my insecurities – and he still motivates me to do my very best. He awakened in me the desire to be a good enough rider and trainer to bring out the best in him! And he can do that just by being himself and enchanting everyone who comes in contact with him.

Shadow and I have been a team for five years already, yet he still manages to make me smile every day, just by being himself.

In this little book, he'll enchant *you* too and make *you* laugh and marvel and think. I know he can do it!

The ugly duckling...

Do you remember the fable about the ugly duckling? The ugly duckling didn't look like his brothers and sisters – he was an outsider. No one wanted to have anything to do with him. This made him very sad because he felt like he was all alone in the world. And then one day his whole family disappeared – they just left him all alone!

The ugly duckling cried bitter tears and searched for his family, but they were nowhere to be found.

But then a beautiful swan saw the little duckling sitting on the edge of the river and quickly swam over to him.

The duckling wondered why such a beautiful creature would come over to him. He was afraid it would just make fun of him. But then he saw the little baby swans that were swimming behind the beautiful mother swan – and they looked just like the ugly duckling!

He wasn't a duck after all – he was a swan! And so the ugly duckling swam off with his new family and grew up into one of the most beautiful swans in all the land. Are you wondering why I'm telling you this story? Because it's also Shadow's story!

But now I'll start at the beginning...

All alone in the world

Shadow was born on April 6, 1995, in Mainz, here in Germany. His astrological sign is Aries, according to the zodiac, and in Native American mythology he is a falcon. We don't know where he's really from, but he was probably separated from his mother very early and passed through countless hands as a foal. I heard that he came from a circus that went bankrupt and then sold all its horses at an auction. Little Shadow and his mother were among them. But the buyer only wanted his mother, so Shadow was sold, which is how he came to be separated from her so early.

We do know what happened to Shadow starting at the age of about two years. A man bought him at a horse market and put him out on the pasture behind his house. That's all there was – just a small meadow. No shelter, no warm stall, and no other horses.

Shadow was all alone. He was fed well every day, but nobody paid any attention to the little horse.

Until, that is, his owner decided to let his two dogs run out on the pasture to join Shadow every morning. Of course, the dogs didn't want to play with Shadow – they wanted to bite him and chase him all over the meadow from sun up until sundown. That went on day after day for almost a year. His owner even thought it was funny to watch Shadow desperately trying to get away from the dogs!

But a friend of the owner didn't find it to be very funny at all. He was afraid that one day Shadow could turn mean.

And that's exactly what happened. One day, Shadow didn't run away. He stayed where he was and attacked the dogs! He got one so badly that it almost died. Once he realized how strong he was, he started going after people, too, without any inhibitions at all!

Soon no one was able to get along with the rowdy animal, and his owner was so frustrated that he wanted to cart the crazy horse off to the nearest slaughterhouse! When Shadow was two

and a half years old, they tried to break him in. But that turned out to be impossible, because Shadow just turned and buried the rider underneath him. He no longer had any respect for people or animals. He was aware of his own strength – and he used it mercilessly.

Shadow goes to reform school

After a lot of talking and arguing, the owner's friend finally convinced him that what Shadow needed was a professional horse trainer to turn him around. They soon found the right person. Dieter Haemmerle at Red Rock Ranch. Dieter is known for his ability to get along with the craziest and most dangerous horses. And he has a policy to never turn down a horse for training.

So they called Dieter…and he agreed to take on Shadow.

But how can you get a horse that is totally wild and hasn't let a person near it in over a year to get into a horse trailer?

Well, you need ten strong men, long ropes and a whole lot of force!

It took five hours, but they somehow managed to get Shadow locked into the trailer and drive quickly south to Red Rock Ranch.

Dieter was looking forward to meeting the horse, which they said was a cross between an Arabian and an Appaloosa.

But when they took down the ramp of the trailer, Dieter was taken aback. The skinny little horse that lay in the transporter had managed to kick his feet through the side of the wagon! During the four-hour drive, the little fellow managed to kick a brand new trailer to bits. He completely demolished it.

Dieter first had to go to work as a carpenter in order to free Shadow from the wrecked wagon. Then it was comparatively easy to get Shadow into a stall, because he was tired from his tantrum in the trailer.

By the time Dieter was done with everything, Shadow's owner was long gone. At the time, Dieter didn't think much of it. He just shrugged his shoulders and decided to take a closer look at his new ward.

"He looked awful," Dieter says today. "He was so thin that you could count his ribs. His coat was shaggy and his hooves were so long that they almost curled upward. Honestly, no one has ever brought me a horse so badly neglected before. I gave him a treatment for worms right on the spot and then made an appointment for shots. I was afraid that he'd bring all kinds of disease to my ranch!"

When Dieter went down to the stable the next day, Shadow was standing in the corridor! Dieter couldn't believe his eyes at first and thought he was dreaming, but during the night Shadow had kicked at the wall of his stall for so long that he'd knocked out the bricks!

The problem child

Dieter is an experienced Western trainer and he learned his trade from the best cowboys in America. He learned how to talk to horses before most people had even heard of the term, "Horse Whisperer."

He took Shadow into the round pen to find out what was wrong with the little fellow.

It didn't take long for Dieter to make a diagnosis: Shadow didn't see people as living beings; for him they were just objects! He ran down anyone who didn't get out of the way quickly enough!

Dieter didn't let Shadow's tricks impress him, though, and he trained every day with him in the round pen until Shadow started to behave a bit more normally. Back then, that meant that he gave a warning *first* and then attacked – which was an improvement over attacking out of the blue. Originally Shadow was supposed to stay three months with Dieter for training, but it soon became clear that this horse needed a lot more time.

At the end of the three months, he had Shadow trained enough that you could lead him, clean him and load him – which was a considerable accomplishment, all things considering! So he called the owner and asked if he wanted to pick Shadow up right away or leave him for more training. Dieter also wanted to be paid for all his work.

But the owner didn't want to pay, and the two men had a serious argument. At the end of it, the owner decided maybe he should take Shadow to the slaughterhouse after all, because the money he'd receive there would at least cover a portion of Dieter's training costs. Or he suggested that Dieter try to sell him to recover his costs. At any rate, the owner didn't want to pay a single penny for the care of his useless, crazy horse.

Dieter was appalled. Shadow had improved tremendously, and now this! He was so upset at this point that he didn't even want to return the young horse to this person. So he said, "Send me the horse's health certificate and identification papers. I'll keep him, and then we're even."

So they had a deal. Only after he hung up did it become clear to Dieter that he had just bought a horse. An almost dangerous, crazy horse, that – at the moment, at least – he couldn't use for riding lessons on the ranch, couldn't use for breeding, and couldn't enter into any big Western tournaments. Dieter didn't know why, but he believed in the goodness of this horse. He was fully convinced that one day Shadow would find "his" person and then become a super horse.

Other trainers just shook their heads and many riders thought Dieter was crazy himself. Still he stuck by his opinion. Shadow would become a Super Horse. It was just a matter of time.

One step forward and two steps back

Dieter spent almost all his free time with Shadow in the round pen or the arena. But he had thirty other horses to take care of! That's not including horse training, lessons, cleaning the stables, feeding the horses, getting hay, repairing fences and so on. Still, even when he was dead tired in the evening and his bones ached, Dieter managed to spend another hour with Shadow.

But things didn't improve; they just got worse, because Shadow learned incredibly quickly! He soon figured out how things worked in the round pen and came up with new ways to outsmart Dieter! He had nothing but nonsense in his head. One day he was frightened by his own shadow and jumped on Dieter's foot.

And now you know how the crazy fellow got his name: Shadow. Both because of how his

speckled skin started showing through his coat, which was getting whiter and whiter – and because he was afraid of his own shadow!

But even with a nice new name and all of Dieter's patience and consistency – it just wasn't working.

"Shadow was the first horse I almost gave up on," admits Dieter today. "I've trained a few hundred horses, broken them in and retrained ones with problems. But this little fellow…he took me to my absolute limits." So Dieter did the only thing he could think of, besides taking Shadow to the slaughterhouse; he took the little gelding and put him out on the paddock with the other horses.

The old Indian trick

Shadow's problem was that before he came under Dieter's care, too many other people had already tried their hands at taming him. A young, "raw" horse that has never had any negative experiences sometimes does dangerous things when it's first being

trained or broken in. If that young horse has never been let down by people, then it quickly stops fooling around and pays attention to the person. But Shadow had no respect for people. He tolerated them if they brought him food, but beyond that, he wanted nothing to do with these strange beings!

Meanwhile, on Dieter's pasture, Shadow became part of a herd for the first time in his life – and he had a hard time trying to find his place among them. He never had the opportunity before to learn how to behave in a herd. At first, he constantly tried to pick fights, and made the others angry. The lead horse soon taught him some manners, however. And Shadow found a loveable buddy in Hotspur, a Haflinger gelding. Hotspur was Dieter's best-trained Western and Trick horse. This odd couple – Hotspur weighed almost twice as much as Shadow – was soon inseparable and, probably for the first time in his life, Shadow experienced friendship and security.

A few weeks went by in which Shadow only saw Dieter when he brought him food. Then Dieter slowly changed his strategy. Every day when he went to the pasture, he greeted the other horses and spent time with them. But he simply ignored Shadow.

The first few weeks Shadow seemed to like that, but after a month went by the little fellow seemed to get curious. He carefully observed

Dieter when he came to the meadow. During the second month, Shadow always stood up at the front of the fence and watched Dieter do his work on the ranch. He was interested, but he didn't really understand what Dieter was really up to – could it be that Dieter truly wanted nothing to do with him?

What Shadow didn't know then, was that Dieter knew all about Indian horse training and was, with endless patience, trying out one of the methods on Shadow.

Long ago, this was how Native Americans used to catch horses: they patiently followed wild horses, sometimes for weeks on end, without pestering them in any way. They just acted as if they weren't really interested in the horse, but just happened to be going the same way. And then, when the Native Americans had the feeling that the time was right, they would just turn around and ride home. And the wild horses would follow them!!

The method works because horses are, by nature, extremely curious. And when they sense that you don't pose a danger to them, they are quick to trust you.

The process doesn't take all that long – no more than eight weeks or so – for a wild horse that has never had a bad experience with a person. But skeptical Shadow took eight months to come around! Every day it was the same procedure; Dieter went to the paddock, greeted the horses and stroked them, took one or the other for training or riding lessons – and acted like the little white horse with the black spots didn't even exist.

After a few months, Shadow came a little closer every day, as if he wanted to find out why the other horses were so happy to see Dieter coming to visit them. Sometimes he followed Dieter around a bit, but he seemed pensive and usually left a lot of space between them. Or he got in the way when Dieter went to stroke another horse, as if to say, "I'm here, too!"

But Dieter just ignored him then or pushed him away.

Then one day Dieter sensed the time had come. He opened the gate to the pasture, went out and waited a moment – and suddenly he felt a horse's muzzle on the back of his neck, nibbling on his hat. He moved on and Shadow followed him – without halter and rope! – onto the ranch while Katja, Dieter's girlfriend, quickly closed the gate. Dieter waited until they reached the grooming area before turning around to stroke Shadow. "So fella, have you finally figured it out?"

And from that day forward, Dieter had a new Shadow on the ranch. Because Shadow followed him, just like a little puppy dog!

New duties

Dieter makes his living off the ranch, which means that all his horses have to join in the work. He decided to teach Shadow to be a schoolmaster.

Shadow, himself, wasn't especially thrilled with the idea. He liked children and was always well behaved around them and didn't try any nonsense. But if an adult wanted to ride him and "show him who's boss," well, look out. It usually didn't take long before Shadow swept through the riding area, bucking and jumping, trying to rid himself of the bothersome rider – and he usually succeeded quickly.

Dieter soon realized that this kind of life was too much for the sensitive horse. Shadow needed one person to focus on. After all, he was always well behaved with Dieter and tried his best to do everything right for him.

But Dieter had 40 horses to take care of on his ranch. He just didn't have enough time to give little Shadow – who now clung to his side – the special attention he needed.

With a heavy heart, Dieter decided it was time to find him a new home. There had to be someone, somewhere, who could be a true friend to Shadow.

The candidates

Dieter didn't just want to sell Shadow to the highest bidder. The person who would get Shadow had to be someone who wouldn't try to break his free spirit. It had to be someone with a lot of patience and understanding – who was also a good rider, because Shadow was everything but easy to manage.

For a good rider like Dieter, he did absolutely everything. Dieter tested him one day in the Western discipline of reining and was amazed. With a little training, Shadow might even manage to beat his top quarter horses!

In other words, he needed skillful, loving hands. But where to find the right person?

It wasn't long before a host of candidates appeared, fascinated by the little wild horse. But Dieter and Katja weren't impressed by any of them: some were heave-ho riders, or people who wanted a fast horse to race around with. A few of them offered Dieter a lot of money for Shadow, but he turned them down because they weren't right for the horse. A troubled child like Shadow should only go to the very best hands.

One day he did sell Shadow, but only on the condition that he could check in later to see how the horse was doing.

The buyer obviously didn't expect him to follow through on that clause, because when Dieter stopped by to visit Shadow one day, he found him in a narrow, dark, cage-like stall. Shadow was deeply disturbed and almost didn't recognize Dieter. Dieter wasted no time; he drove straight home, hooked up the horse trailer, and when he returned he thrust the money back into the buyer's hands and took Shadow back to the ranch.

It took many weeks before Shadow calmed down again. Dieter's entire training was almost out the window – he was back at square one with many disciplines. Shadow was fearful every time he even glimpsed a crop and his whole body trembled when someone made hectic movements. We still don't know what happened to him during his time with the new owner, but for a long time Shadow panicked any time he saw a dark stall – something that still happens occasionally.

Dieter decided not to make any more compromises. If he had to, he'd keep Shadow at Red Rock Ranch as a show horse. He would only sell him to a person when he was 100% certain that it was the right person.

The phone call

I had just finished my first book in 1999, *Horses of the World – Course Horses*, for a German publisher…and the check arrived. I finally had enough money to fulfill a lifelong dream – having my own horse. I've been riding since I was three years old, and started learning Western riding with Dieter when I was fifteen. I was so fascinated by this style of riding that there was only one kind of horse that would do – a Western horse.

I didn't want anything out of the ordinary, just a lovable, devoted horse that I could do anything with.

So I gave Dieter a call, because I knew that he always had a few horses to sell.

"Have I got a horse for you!" he said when he heard me describe my dream horse. "Shadow would be perfect for you!"

"You don't mean *the* Shadow, do you?" I remembered the wild horse that almost ran me down when I photographed him for Dieter last year.

"I sure do. He's four years old now and has changed a lot. Why don't you come by and take a look at him? Believe me, he's the horse for you."

I wasn't too sure about that. I had no experience with a horse that young, and didn't have much faith in my ability to ride a horse like Shadow, much less train him.

But Dieter worked so hard to convince me that I figured it wouldn't hurt to just take a look.

The first encounter

It was January 13, 2000, and it was a cold and rainy day.

Dieter was exuding happiness when he greeted me, and took me straight to the paddock.

And there he was, covered with a torn horse blanket that was much too big for him. The only white that you could see under all the dirt were his ears. Shadow moved nervously from side to side. He seemed tensed almost to the breaking point and never let us out of his sight.

"Go on over to him– just go!" Dieter shoved me right up to the gate and I figured that I had to be polite and greet the horse…

Shadow suddenly calmed down, leaned his head to the side and looked at me. Then he put his nose close to me, sniffed and rubbed his head against my cheek.

CLICK!

I heard the click in my head. It was a feeling that went through me, body and soul. *This is the one!*

It was as if Shadow had always been a part of me. It felt like I was being reunited with my long-lost best friend.

A few years later, when we celebrated our fifth anniversary together, a friend of mine said that Shadow and I really must be kindred souls. And another friend put together a horoscope for

Shadow and me, which showed that we fit together perfectly.

On that nasty, rainy winter's day, I remember how fascinated I was by the powerful aura of this horse. He radiated something that I've perceived in very few horses indeed.

When I turned around, Dieter was grinning from ear to ear.

"So, should we unpack him and take him out for a spin?"

Suddenly I came to my senses. Such a young, wild horse? – No. There was no way I could manage that.

"Er, Dieter..."

But once Dieter gets something in his head, it's hard to talk him out of it. Before I knew what was happening, we were standing in the riding arena and Dieter was lunging Shadow.

I got a funny feeling in the pit of my stomach. Shadow was fast – very fast. And he was wild. This couldn't possibly work out.

But then Dieter attached a rope to his halter, swung himself up on Shadow's bare back and rode a few rounds with him. It was amazing to watch. Shadow was clearly nervous and about to explode – but he was also extremely sensitive and he responded to the smallest signal.

"You'll see. One day you'll understand each other so well that you'll only have to think a command and he'll do it!" said Dieter, as he backed him into place and dismounted. "Come on, give it a try – or do you want a saddle?"

You've got to hand it to Dieter – he has a very good sense of which person fits with which horse. Back then, however, I just wasn't confident enough with the situation.

On the other hand, I figured I should give it a try, or maybe I'd miss the chance of a lifetime.

And it was strange. I felt *right* sitting there on Shadow's bare back. He responded sensitively to me and really tried hard to do everything right. I started off riding some figures, sideways and backwards, and then decided to give Shadow a real "test ride."

We went back to the grooming station, where I brushed off the coating of dirt on his coat and then saddled him up.

We went back into the arena and Dieter gave me a few "instructions for use." Shadow was visibly nervous. Suddenly all the horses on the pasture next to the arena started to gallop together, and it was all I could do to keep him from leaping over the fence.

But he quickly calmed down, and then Dieter left us alone.

"Take your time getting to know each other," he said and swung himself onto his tractor and rode off. He had more faith in my abilities than I did!

I rode Shadow around the arena for a while, then dismounted and led him to the grooming station. I didn't feel comfortable all alone with a strange horse , but fortunately Katja suddenly appeared and offered to take me around.

"If I tell you what a crazy horse he used to be,

you'd never believe me," she said and began recounting some of Shadow's earlier escapades.

I felt even more uneasy about buying a horse like that. "What if he relapses into his old behavior?"

"He won't, believe me. If he had anything against you, you'd be under him already."

And as if on cue, hundreds of crows suddenly flapped over the pasture, squawking loudly over our heads. Katja's Haflinger bolted and Shadow shot off like an arrow. Although he was clearly spooked, I was able to slow him down after just ten galloping leaps with a gentle, "Whoa!" His whole body trembled from fright, but he tried to calm himself down and listen to me.

Dieter waited for us at the grooming station.

"Well? *Well*?"

"What do you mean, 'Well'?"

He rolled his eyes.

"Shadow is perfect for you, isn't he? He likes you! Well? Well?"

I sighed, dismounted, and almost before I touched the ground, Shadow nudged his head against my shoulder and wanted to be stroked.

"It looks like Shadow's already made his decision!" laughed Katja.

"I'd really like to sell him to you," said Dieter. "With you, I know he'd have a good life and you would treat him with respect. I don't want to be forced to sell him to someone who wouldn't take good care of him. And here with me, he'd have to work as a school master, but that would destroy him psychologically."

"How much do you want for him?"

Dieter scratched his head, "Hmmn, well, if I take into consideration how much the little fellow has cost me already…but if you take him and promise that he'll live in a good stable, where he can go out to the pasture every day… and you won't sell him to anyone else…well, then you can have him at my cost."

In other words, he gave him to me for practically nothing! When I think about what Dieter normally charges for one of his horses…well, it was even more obvious how fond he was of this horse.

"Okay. But let's bring him to the clinic for a thorough checkup first, just to be sure."

"Sure," said Dieter. "I'll call them right now and make an appointment for tomorrow."

When I drove home that evening I was so happy, and I immediately called my family and told them about my new acquisition. They weren't exactly thrilled. A horse? But that's so expensive, what was I thinking, and so on and so forth…

But it didn't matter to me. It was my horse. And my decision.

Bad news

The next morning, Dieter brought Shadow to the nearby horse clinic where he had a full examination.

I wanted to be totally confident that Shadow was in good health.

The team of physicians was smitten with the little gelding, and Shadow was very cooperative, allowing them to complete all their tests: blood test, lunging on different surfaces, x-rays, bending and running free.

Four hours later, my phone rang.

"Hello?"

"Hi, it's Dieter."

Oh, no, I thought, something must be wrong. I could hear it in his voice.

"What's wrong with Shadow?"

"There's something on his back. They aren't sure yet what it is yet, but the veterinarian wants to talk to you himself to explain it. I'll drop Shadow off at the ranch now. You can meet me there in an hour and then we can drive over to the clinic together, okay?"

"Sure. I'm on my way."

As soon as I hung up the receiver, I got a sick feeling in my stomach. What if it were something serious? Could I afford to take care of a sick horse for years and years and cover all the veterinarian bills? Would I be able to ride him at all?

All too often I had seen friends buy a sick horse out of sympathy and then not have enough money for his therapy and medication. Eventually they would have to sell him to a dealer or a slaughterhouse. I wanted to spare Shadow all that, and during the long drive to Freiburg from Sasbachwalden. I decided it would be better if I didn't take Shadow after all…

The veterinarian was very pleasant and he showed me the complete report of Shadow's physical. They checked absolutely everything and Shadow was in perfect health – except for two things.

The vet showed me x-rays of Shadow's back. On one x-ray, you could see that two of his vertebrae were a little closer together than they should be.

"It *isn't* kissing spine," the doctor said emphatically. "And if the horse is always trained correctly, not excessively, then it won't turn into that. It's also possible that it will go away by itself. But there is an outside chance that it could develop into Kissing Spine."

With Kissing Spine, the vertebrae come into contact with each other, causing the horse tremendous pain. Horses like that can never be ridden again.

I felt myself losing hope.

"And what else is there?"

"He has a slight cough. A lot of horses have one this time of year, but there's a risk, however slight, that any cough can turn chronic."

"What's the worst case scenario?"

"If both conditions occur – and we're talking about the absolute worst possible case – then in a year or two he'll have to take early retirement."

I saw my dream collapsing and felt tears shoot into my eyes. Great. I finally found something that truly made me happy – and now this.

We rode back in silence. Dieter was as shocked as I was by the diagnosis. He had no idea that his cheerful joker could be afflicted with so serious a condition. You'd never know it by looking at him.

"The decision is up to you," he said.

"If you'd like, then I'll give you a full money back guarantee for the next six months. If his back goes or he starts to cough, then you can bring him back and I'll give you another horse in exchange."

"Nonsense, Dieter, you know that I'd never do anything like that. When I make a decision, then I stick to it…That said, I don't think this will work out."

"No problem," said Dieter quickly. But I could hear the disappointment in his voice.

When we got back to the ranch, I saw Shadow prancing on his paddock. He looked over to me, full of expectation.

I tried to get away from the ranch before someone noticed the tears in my eyes…

A difficult decision

I just made it home before I broke down in sobs. I didn't really understand why I had gotten so emotional. I mean, it was just a horse – and not even my own!

I went online to research horse coughs and the Kissing Spine syndrome. Then I called a few friends and experts to ask their advice. About half said to take him and the other half said not to take him at any price.

The next day, I drove with my friend, Concetta, to see the horse dealer from whom she had bought Little Joe, her Criollo.

"I'm sure you'll find one there that you like," she said.

I looked at more than fifty horses and test rode ten of them. But I couldn't get Shadow out of my head. Although each of the horses was nice and special in its own way, none of them could hold a candle to Shadow.

On the way back, Concetta remarked, "Our outing was something of a success, wasn't it?"

"What are you talking about? I still don't have a horse!"

She smiled. "Of course you do…and now it's finally clear to you!"

When I got home, I called the only people I hadn't yet asked for advice because they didn't know anything about horses – my parents.

"What will happen to Shadow now?" asked my mother.

"I have no idea. Maybe Dieter will find someone who'll buy him anyway."

"Is his condition so serious that he's in pain?"

"At this point, he's okay. And it doesn't have to get worse."

"Well," said my mother, "look at it like this: Your back is a little crooked, too. You have a curvature of the spine. That's the same thing, it seems to me. So what? You're still alive. No one's health is 100% perfect. And because you have a similar condition you're in a better position to understand what needs to be done to keep it under control."

"Is he a nice horse?" asked my dad.

"Oh yes. He's just great. A little nervous, but a really nice fellow."

"Well, what are you waiting for? Take him! Who knows if you'll ever find another one like him!"

I hung up immediately and called Dieter right away.

"So you've finally come to your senses?"

I had to smile. Sometimes I get the feeling that he can read minds.

"Yes, Dieter, I'll take him."

"Terrific, I'm relieved. Just a second… Kaaaatttjjaaaa?"

"Yes?"

"She'll take him!!!"

"Well, fin-a-lly!!"

Concetta was right. Shadow was my horse before I even realized it myself.

Shadow is my horse!

My investment advisor was a little shocked when I made an appointment with him on January 25, 2000, and instructed him to give me all my savings.

"But you're making money, and the stock market is rising," he argued.

"I don't care, I need the money right away!" Half an hour later, I was on my way to Dieter's ranch, with the contract – and a wad of money in my pocket.

Dieter and Katja greeted me with big smiles.

"You won't regret it. Believe me, Shadow is *your* horse; you were made for each other.

In the house, we signed the contract and I gave Dieter the money. We agreed that Shadow would remain on the ranch for another six weeks until construction of the stables where I wanted to keep him was completed. This gave Shadow and me a chance to get to know each other better first. And Dieter could continue training him a bit.

Once the official business was complete, the three of us went down to the paddock and I greeted my new acquisition with a carrot.

"He looks like a wild boar right now," said Katja, in that dry manner of hers. "But believe me, in five years he'll be a top achiever. What

he really needs is someone who can lavish attention on him – and give him huge portions of fodder."

"What kind of a breed is he anyway?" I asked.

"I have no idea. I think he's part Arabian. We don't have any papers for him, just his health certificate."

"It doesn't really matter, he's perfect the way he is!"

"Well, congratulations – now you're a horse mama!"

That afternoon, I spent a lot of time with Shadow. I picked him up at the paddock and led him to the grooming station and gave him a thorough grooming. Then I sat with him and stroked him. Shadow seemed totally fascinated – he wasn't used to a person giving him so much attention.

Later I drove over to the farm where I planned to keep him. Two years ago, Kiera – the horse I share – moved in there, so I'm over there practically every day. At the time, it was the only farm in the whole area that offered stalls and paddocks. When I first told him I was looking for a horse, the owner had just begun building ten more stalls and he promised to reserve one for me.

We agreed that Shadow would move to the farm on March 10th, my birthday.

That evening I asked a few friends to celebrate with me – and to help me put together a list of all the things I would be needing for Shadow. It was a very long list. So the next day, I went to the bank and cleaned out the rest of my account!

Six weeks at Red Rock Ranch

Every weekend, and as often as my work allowed during the week, I drove the 40 miles to Dieter's ranch to visit Shadow. At the beginning, I didn't even ride him very much, just went into the round pen with him and did some ground work. Ground work had helped me win Kiera's trust when I first started with her and I never had any trouble later when I rode her. That says a lot because she often rebelled and tried to throw her owner and those who subsequently rode her. Kiera is a very sensitive horse and Shadow is even more sensitive. That's why I gave him a lot of time to get to know me on the ground back then in the winter of 2000.

It turned out to be the right thing to do, because we ran into a lot of difficulties from the very beginning. Sometimes Shadow just ripped the lunge out of my hands and ran off or reared up at me if he didn't feel like training.

A few days after Shadow officially became mine, Concetta and her husband Joerg accompanied me to Red Rock Ranch to meet my horse. As usual, Joerg had his camera with him and took the first pictures of Shadow and me together. When I look at the photos today, I can only shake my head. What could I possibly have seen in that skinny, shaggy, crazy horse?

Probably the same thing that Concetta and Joerg saw when they met Shadow.

"A perfect fit!" was Joerg's first comment.

"He needs a whole lot of love," said Concetta.

"And even more to eat," commented Joerg wryly. Right after our visit to the ranch he took me to the nearest feed store where I bought a huge sack of mash. Although Dieter gave him twice as big a ration as the other horses got, Shadow didn't gain any weight and his coat was shaggy and his hooves were brittle.

"I'm convinced it's psychological with him," said Katja. "If you're unhappy, then you get sick easily and don't have any appetite. Shadow knows that something is missing in his life."

But what? I asked myself. Until one day I saw what Shadow did when I gave him a cough drop. He rolled his tongue and sucked on it with great pleasure.

That's something that foals do when their mothers suckle them. It was obvious to me that something went wrong in Shadow's life when he was very young. But how could I find out what it was? We didn't know anything at all about his early life.

"Give him some time," said Dieter again and again. "He's a terrific horse, believe me, even if the others don't see that yet. He'll be a real star one day – I know he will!"

It was true that most of my friends weren't exactly thrilled with Shadow. Some of them thought I was crazy and couldn't understand what it was that I saw in my horse. They all thought he was "nice," but that's all. "He'll be okay for rides when he calms down a bit, but not much more," was the general opinion of him.

Back then I used to pay a lot more attention to the opinions of other people, and their comments made me sad. Still, Dieter, Katja, Joerg and Concetta encouraged me and offered to help when I ran into trouble. Joerg looked around for a suitable saddle and Concetta showed me where I could get a good price on feed. Dieter and Katja were always there for me with advice and hands-on help. Without them, I could hardly have managed those first six weeks with Shadow!

One day, Concetta and I took Shadow for a walk, and it was the first time I caught a glimpse of what kind of a temper my horse could have. When he was tired of walking around and I scolded him to go on, he reared up on his hind legs and attacked me without warning! He had accepted Dieter as boss and behaved around him, but I would have to work hard to earn his respect. That meant I had a lot of work to do!

Shadow arrives!

On March 10th, at the crack of dawn, the telephone rang. Oh great, I thought; I can't even sleep in on my 22nd birthday.

"Good morning, it's Dieter calling to wish you a happy birthday!"

When Dieter told me that he'd be bringing Shadow over in two hours – a bit earlier than we had originally planned – I was suddenly wide awake.

No problem. I quickly got dressed and dashed out of the house to go to the stable.

I purposely didn't tell many people that Shadow would be arriving on that day because the people at the stable tend to be extremely curious. I wanted Shadow to be able to ease into his new life here slowly.

Imagine my surprise when I saw Concetta and Joerg in front of Shadow's new stall, setting up a champagne breakfast on my feedbox!

"Don't look at me like that – you know there's nothing I don't know about you!" she said and wished me a happy birthday. She never told me how she found out that Shadow was coming that day.

The owner of the farm had prepared everything for Shadow's arrival. Fresh straw covered the floor of the stall and there was a big pile of hay in the corner. The only thing missing was Shadow.

A few minutes later, a big jeep pulling a horse trailer, with "Red Rock Ranch" emblazoned on the side, drove around the corner.

Shadow was tense to the breaking point when Dieter led him out of the trailer. He was so excited that he stumbled, and then hastily rushed down the rest of the ramp. Then he stood still for a moment and, with his head held high, he whinnied tentatively.

The ten other horses in the stable answered him, and then we all took turns greeting the new arrival. The farm owner's wife slipped out quietly and returned with a huge serving of freshly soaked barley, which she poured into Shadow's trough.

"So, little fella, we're going to fatten you up!" she said resolutely and started off by giving Shadow twice the ration the other horses received.

Meanwhile, Dieter was already out surveying the entire farm. After his experience the first time he sold Shadow, Dieter had become extremely cautious. He started asking the owner of the farm a slew of questions: how many acres of pasture land he had, what he planted there, how often the horses go out there, where he gets his hay and barley, how often the horses are fed, how often their stalls are cleaned and so on…After half an hour of questioning, Dieter seemed satisfied.

Next we wanted to get Shadow acquainted with his paddock neighbor, Concetta's gelding,

Little Joe. Since it wouldn't have been a good idea to introduce them in the narrow confines of the paddock, we led them both out to the riding arena – and all of us were relieved to see how the older Criollo gelding and Shadow got along instantly. After establishing the ranking order, they began to play together. Joe acted like a favorite uncle, showing the little boy around the new neighborhood. Shadow bonded happily with the sweet pinto.

For Dieter and Katja, the time had come to start heading back. After all, they had 39 horses and a bunch of riding students waiting for them back at the ranch.

And then I noticed that Dieter was a little sad. He was having a hard time saying goodbye to Shadow, even though he knew that he'd still be seeing him quite often. Of course, the difference now was that he was no longer *his* little problem child.

Katja's eyes teared up when she said goodbye to her former ward, and then the two of them drove off sadly.

That evening I got together with Concetta, Joerg and my other friends at a little restaurant to celebrate my birthday – and once again, Concetta took care of everything. Joerg put a huge package on the floor in front of me. It was so big I could hardly lift it myself. The box was filled to the brim with carrots, horse treats and all the things a horse needs: brush, comb,

sponge, mane detangling spray, blue spray, hoof grease, halter, rope and more…

My 22nd birthday is one I'll never forget!

Our first spring

Shadow needed time to become accustomed to his new home. His first few weeks there were not easy, especially since the horses in the nearby paddocks didn't particularly like him. I

tried to give him time to settle in and just sat near him in the paddock and observed him. After a few days, once he quieted down, I took the bridle, attached a rope to it and took Shadow on his first walk through his new neighborhood. Shadow was visibly nervous – little things startled him at first, but after a while he calmed down. On the way back, I heard a clank and then the rope went limp. I turned around slowly and saw that the hook on the bridle, where the rope had been attached, had broken – and Shadow stood there, totally free, looking at me with wide-open eyes! I reached out my hand to him and he obediently walked toward me and allowed me to tie on the rope. We both recovered quickly from our mutual shock and continued our walk.

When there was work to be done, however, my little roughneck behaved totally differently. He fought tooth and nail to avoid lunging, and regularly tore himself away from me and marched off proudly, head and tail held high, acting like he wanted to stick out his tongue at me.

All of us at the stable had a lot of fun with Shadow that spring and summer because he was always up to something silly. He refused, for instance, to drink out of his own trough and always went to Joe's box across the way to get a drink. And if the farmer didn't pay attention to him when he cleaned out the stalls, Shadow snuck past him and then pranced in the corridor past the other stalls.

Once we were able to establish (more or less) that I was the one in charge on the ground, I started riding Shadow bareback in the arena. In the beginning he reacted tentatively, probably because I gave signals differently than Dieter did, but he tried hard to do what I wanted. Galloping was a real problem for him, though. On the right side, he couldn't gallop at all and on the left he constantly slipped into an uneven canter. We had a lot of work ahead of us!

Concetta and Little Joe accompanied me on my first few rides with Shadow. And I was glad of it, because Dieter rarely took Shadow off the ranch. As a result, he was afraid of just about everything. It was like running the gauntlet, but Joe's stoicism helped to prevent the worst!

The bee sting

In the summer of 2000, Shadow met Beauty, Astrid's crossbreed mare, and was instantly smitten. We often let them run together in the riding arena. One day, when I rode out with Karen, who shared Beauty, Shadow suddenly started to act crazy. He reared up and then bucked and kicked wildly so that it was almost impossible to hold him. I scolded him and finally he stopped but he looked very uncomfortable as we walked back. Then when I took off the saddle, I saw it – something had bitten Shadow in his belly, right under the girth. The bite seemed to swell up before my eyes. I called the veterinarian immediately.

"Oh my, it'll take quite awhile for this to heal. No saddle for the next six months," he said when he saw it, and gave Shadow some medication.

When he returned several weeks later for a follow-up exam, he noticed that part of the stinger was still stuck in the wound. Only after the entire stinger was extracted could the wound begin to heal.

That meant I could only ride bareback – or not at all. Since I didn't want to put Shadow out to pasture for six months, I decided to try it without a saddle. And you know what? It worked out great! In retrospect, I have to say that being forced to ride without a saddle was the best thing that could have happened, because now Shadow and I don't need one at all anymore. And I learned how to handle myself in any situation without needing a saddle.

Because I couldn't ride every day, I started to work with Shadow on circus exercises in the arena. The effect was astonishing – Shadow was a changed horse. He didn't fool around anymore – instead he was quite eager to learn.

He didn't understand the Spanish trot at first, and always looked at me with questioning eyes when I tapped his leg, as if to say, "I know you want me to do *something*. I just don't know what it is!"

Somewhere along the line we succeeded, and soon Shadow could do the Spanish walk, the curtsy bow, and stand on his hind legs. Since he was always rearing up on his hind legs when he scuffled with his buddies out on the pasture, I decided to make a trick command out of it in order to keep it under my control. At any rate, Shadow always enjoyed our circus training and made progress very quickly!

Since I couldn't spend time with Shadow every day, I asked my friend Denise to help out, and she took him for longer rides a few times a week. Denise was an accomplished rider and Shadow's crazy little moves barely got a reaction from her.

The first show

Sometime in late August I got a phone call from Dieter. He told me that he planned to host one of his legendary open houses at the ranch. Dieter asked me to bring Shadow and give a short performance with him.

I wasn't sure whether that was such a good idea. After all, I had only had Shadow for half a year, and to be honest, there wasn't all that much that we could do yet.

But Dieter kept at me until I finally agreed. And he promised to pick up Shadow and me since I had neither a horse trailer, nor a car to pull one with.

A week before the show, Katja drove over to pick up Shadow and all his equipment. The next day, I drove out to Red Rock Ranch and found Shadow out at pasture, hanging out with

his old friends. I guess it was like a homecoming for him.

Then Dieter and I worked out a script for the first show of my entire life!

Nothing too elaborate, just a little groundwork and then a few circus tricks. But I was very excited, especially when I saw what the others were presenting. On Saturday just before the show, it suddenly hit me. While I had taken care of just about everything for the show, there was one important element that I had overlooked completely – I didn't have a special outfit for the show!

I asked Katja if she knew of anyone who could lend me something at the last minute. She pointed out a small trailer that had been parked on the meadow for the past week.

"Just ask for Jessy. She's probably got a whole closet full of costumes in there!"

So I went over and a young woman, maybe three or four years younger than myself, came out to talk to me.

"No problem!" she laughed as she pulled me into her trailer. She threw open the door of her closet and said, "Take a look and pick out whichever you like!"

"Jessy" was Jessica Maria Scholz, a very successful young Western rider – in fact, two weeks after this show, she went on to win the European Championship in the Western Trail Youth category! At the ranch she'd be performing with her pony, El Amigo. Jessy had a lot of experience and I was grateful to her for giving me a few tips for my own performance. Making friends with other Western riders is really easy!

The next day, the day of the show, was a beautiful late summer day – the sky was a gorgeous blue and there was a light breeze. It was simply perfect, which is, no doubt, what the 1000 spectators, who came from far and wide, thought.

Katja was very encouraging, but I got more and more nervous as I waited to go out with Shadow to the riding arena.

Although our performance wasn't perfect at our first show, it was obvious that Shadow genuinely enjoyed himself. Some horses love to show off to an audience and seem to know that the applause is praise for them. Horses like that are few and far between, but Shadow is definitely one of them.

Dieter nearly burst with pride for his former problem child. After my performance, he was so excited that he swung himself up on Shadow's bare back and told the audience about this horse's unbelievable story – what a crazy horse he had been just one year ago!

A riding hall just for us!

It was a cold, rainy winter. We frequently had freezing rain that turned the ground into a sheet of ice. The riding arena on the farmstead, which wasn't in very good condition to begin with, was absolutely useless in this weather. All the paths in and around the village were iced over, too – only the streets were okay. I had no other choice than to carefully walk Shadow through the village to the indoor riding hall in town, in order to get a little exercise.

At first Shadow was afraid of the hall and didn't even want to go in – after all, he had no way of knowing what it would be like inside. So the first few days, I didn't ride him at all there, to let him adjust. Fortunately, the riding club had two halls, and the smaller one was almost always empty. It was about 70-80 feet long and was originally conceived as a lunging arena. In this extremely conservative club, people didn't think too much of ground training, so Shadow and I usually had the place to ourselves. Once I had him trained on the lunge here, I could even let him run freely around the hall. Shadow loved having a place to run around – and this was really the only place to do it at this time of year, because even his paddock was iced over. After

ten sessions in the smaller hall, Shadow still didn't feel much like letting me ride him. So I decided to continue with the circus exercises, since I had the whole winter – and the whole hall to work with him. I stuffed my pockets full of horse treats, took the lunge line and crop, and continued practicing the curtsy.

The Curtsy and Kneel

I wanted Shadow to first learn how to curtsy, and then we could develop kneeling from that. It took a while, but eventually Shadow understood what I wanted him to do and then started to work into the position himself when I cued him with the crop. I practiced the curtsy on both sides until Shadow was confident with the move.

Then one day I prompted him to do the curtsy on the right side, and as soon as he was halfway down, I cued his left leg. Shadow clumsily bent this leg too and kneeled down at a precarious slant. I allowed him to stand up immediately and praised him profusely. Then we called it a day.

A few days later when we were practicing again, I noticed that whenever he tried to kneel, his back legs were always at an angle. No wonder we weren't getting anywhere with the exercise. I decided that I needed to back up and work on the mountain goat position first, so that Shadow could learn to kneel more elegantly.

The exhausting mountain goat

In this exercise, the horse positions its legs close together under his belly, as if he were a mountain goat standing on a narrow cliff, hence the name. It's an extremely strenuous exercise, but it's excellent for developing the horse's sense of balance. Since it forces the horse to arch his back, it's also very good for horses with back problems.

At first Shadow was annoyed when I began to touch his back legs, and he lashed out at me a few times. After a while he began to understand what I wanted and lifted his legs when I cued them with my crop. All I had to do now was explain to him that he also had to move the back legs forward. But how? And more importantly, how could I teach him to keep his front legs in position while moving up the back ones? The natural reaction to this signal would be to walk off!

This exercise looks so simple once the horse has mastered it, but it's the most time-consuming one to teach.

Finally I came up with a solution. I put my hand on Shadow's chest and then touched him with the crop. When he lifted a back leg, I used my foot to push it forward a bit and encouraged him to set it down there. When Shadow understood what I wanted, we worked at it, inch by inch. It's like doing a split. You can't do one the first time you try, and you could even hurt yourself if you do. You need to do it step by step. And so, over the course of just a week, Shadow learned to move his legs closer and closer together until his front and back hooves touched each other. He learned to hold this position for a quite a while and felt good doing it. At first it was so exhausting for him that the muscles in his hindquarters began to twitch – a clear sign that it was still too much for him. To strengthen his muscles, I lunged him a lot, sometimes with a chambon, a strap that encourages the horse to move forward, and sometimes over ground poles.

The greatest gift

One day I decided to try again with kneeling. Shadow had gotten much stronger and had improved his balance with the Mountain Goat – maybe he'd be ready for kneeling. So I gave him the command and then cued his back legs. But my plan went awry. Shadow did a brief kneel, but my cueing his hind legs confused him and he almost tipped over towards me!

Suddenly I had a great idea. I let him get up. Then I gave him the command to kneel without touching his hindquarters and he kept himself relatively erect. I left it at that one attempt, but decided to try something else the next day.

When we began practicing the next day, I took two ropes and tied them to his halter –

like reins. Then I cued him to kneel. He got down obediently and waited. I reached for one of the reins and carefully turned his head away from me, simultaneously cuing his hind legs. He hesitated briefly, but then, with a quiet grunt, he got down all the way and lay down before me. He didn't jump up, either. Instead, he turned his head to me and looked me in the eyes as if to say, "Aren't I clever?"

I sat down next to him and praised him, stroking him and giving him horse treats. He waited a few more minutes before trying to get up. I stepped back and then gave him the sign for "up!" He stood up again, shook himself and then came straight to me.

What happened to my hysterical horse? I didn't understand why, but Shadow was suddenly calm and relaxed. The change in him was amazing. I gave him some more treats and then we headed home. Back at the stables I didn't tell anyone about my amazing discovery – no one would have believed me anyway. At best they would have laughed at me and made fun of me. So I decided to keep the experience to myself. Lying down is the greatest gift a horse can give to a person. By doing that he shows that he completely trusts that person. And to be honest, I didn't want to share such a special moment with anyone else in the world. Shadow had given me a gift that I wanted to keep all to myself.

The cuddly fellow

We also practiced other exercises that winter. Circus training made up just a small part of our program. Shadow had an uneven pace in all of the basic gaits, and I wanted to spend the winter helping him overcome this with a lot of lunging and cavaletti work. Unfortunately, Shadow found these exercises dull, so I never spent more than twenty minutes at a time on them. In between, we practiced the circus exercises for fifteen or twenty minutes. Shadow's favorite move was lying down. And since he liked to lie down for a while, I'd go over to him and sit down next to him. He seemed to like that even more.

One day, I sat down cross-legged next to him and before I knew what was happening, Shadow lifted his head, looked into my eyes and then lay his head down in my lap, as if it were the most normal thing in the world for him to do! He grunted happily, closed his eyes – and tried to fall asleep!

I couldn't believe my eyes. When I think about how many years – not to mention the brutal methods some use – most trainers need to teach a horse to lie down, it becomes even more incredible to me that Shadow would do it of his own free will! Simply because he wanted to!

Shadow repositioned his head in my lap a few times to get more comfortable and hummed peacefully. I started massaging his forehead and he closed his eyes again. I don't know how long we stayed in that position, but I do know that after a while, my legs fell asleep. A sudden shooting pain in my hip forced me, with a heavy heart, to push Shadow away before his 65-pound head pinched a nerve. Shadow grumbled discontentedly, but then he sat up without further complaint and waited obediently for me to give him the command to get up. I was dazed as we walked home together.

That evening I called Dieter to tell him what had happened – I was curious to hear what he would say. There was a big silence at first and I was afraid that I had somehow made him angry.

"Dieter, is something wrong?" I was uneasy. Could it be that Shadow did that because he was sick? Who knew?

But then Dieter chuckled softly. "No, no. Now everything is right!" is what Dieter said. "The little fellow finally found his person. That's the biggest gift any horse can give."

Shadow learns trail, Spring 2001

Even the most brutal winter eventually comes to an end, and Mother Nature rewarded us with a beautiful, warm spring. Shadow clearly enjoyed the nice weather and romped about on his paddock. I hoped that the farmer would soon allow him onto the pasture, especially since the horses at nearby stables were already out. But the farmer kept coming up with new excuses for not letting the horses out – first he said there was too much grass, then too little, then it was too hot, then too cold or too damp or too dry.

I had no choice but to work out with Shadow

every day and take him riding to give him a release for his pent-up energy. The wound on his belly had healed and left a scar. Hair would never grow over it, but if I used a special neoprene western girth, then saddling him up to ride would be no problem.

No problem, that is, except for the nonsense he thought up every time we were riding off the premises of the farmstead. Shadow always seemed to be shy toward everything and everyone – or acted that way, at least, constantly testing my reactions.

It really wasn't easy managing him, so I tried to give him other things to think about, so that he didn't have too big an opportunity to fool around.

I started practicing Trail with him. The Western discipline of Trail comes from the daily riding cowboys do when they work. The horses have to cross wooden bridges, open a gate without letting go of it, trot over poles, walk over plastic sheeting, go backwards around a corner and much more.

Shadow took to our trail training with great fervor, just as he had with circus training, which we also continued at least three times a week. Funny, sometimes I got the feeling that a few of these exercises were simply too easy for him. Trotting aimlessly around a pen drove him crazy. He wanted more than physical exercise, he wanted a mental challenge!

And that's exactly what Trail, which is con-sidered the single most important discipline in a tournament, gave him.

In just a few weeks, Shadow learned so much and so quickly, that I was running out of ideas for new exercises! He couldn't perform anything perfectly, but it was obvious that he really thought about each movement, and how best to do it. I had so much fun working with him that the spring just flew by!

Vacation at the ox stable

A warm spring is often followed by a hot summer – and the summer of 2001 was very hot.

But that wasn't the only problem. Because the stable was located near a floodplain, we had a big problem with mosquitoes. That summer it seemed like zillions of mosquitoes and horseflies hatched in the nearby ponds and streams. Horseflies are big and extremely aggressive insects. When they sting, it doesn't just itch, it really hurts and swells quickly.

Believe it or not, our farmer suddenly had the bright idea to force the horses to stay out at pasture – at the hottest time of year when the bugs were biting.

At first I thought Shadow was just being silly, standing out in the middle of the pasture with the sun beating down on him and the mosquitoes swarming, instead of walking over to the protection of his cool stall. But then one day I noticed that the stall gates that led to the pasture were locked. There was an obvious reason for this. We were responsible for taking care of the pasture, while the farmer was in charge of cleaning the stalls. Keeping the horses at pasture saved him a lot of work.

From past experience, I knew that talking to him about this situation would lead nowhere, but the horses were covered with so many insect bites that their backs looked like coffeecakes. So I decided to take Shadow on vacation for the next two months. My family had a mountain cabin just below the Hornisgrinde peak, about 3,200 feet above sea level. The air was cool up there, about 10 degrees lower than where I lived – and there were no mosquitoes or horseflies.

Back then I didn't have a horse trailer, so I asked the farmer if he'd lend me his. It was no problem, and he even helped me to get Shadow in and load up everything I needed for our vacation. Then we drove off on our adventure.

Shadow was quite confused when we arrived and was all stiff as he walked out of the trailer. He stood in the middle of the parking lot and whinnied shrilly. When he didn't hear any horses answer him back, he got a little uneasy.

I led him to his new stable. It was originally built as a night camp for the oxen that were used to clear wood. As a result, it wasn't as high as horse stables normally are, but it was built out of concrete and pleasantly cool inside.

Once Shadow finally understood that there were no other horses around, he accepted it and calmed down. I tied a ladder in front of the sliding gate to the stable so that he would be able to look out into the courtyard.

Every day I took Shadow on two or three big rides through the mountains. I knew my way around the area by foot – after all, this is where

I grew up – but getting around is very different when you're on a horse.

One day, on our way back from a lake, I remembered there was a shortcut to the stables through a ravine called Beaver Gulch. If we took that route, we'd be back in an hour.

I walked that trail years ago, but back then I was still a little girl and I remembered it to be much wider than it was in reality!

The path grew narrower and narrower and the ravine grew steeper and steeper. By the time I realized that I had taken us into a trap, the path was so narrow that there wasn't enough room to turn Shadow around. I had no choice but to dismount and lead the way – and hope that he didn't take a false step.

We walked the serpentine path along the cliff's sheer edge down into the chasm. Sometimes rain or snow causes chunks of rock to loosen and fall onto the narrow path, making it even more precarious. Someone out hiking can climb over them if he's careful, but when I turned a corner with Shadow and saw a huge granite boulder blocking the way in front of us, I realized our situation did not look good at all. My thoughts raced as I tried to figure out what to do, while Shadow calmly grazed next to me. He seemed to find the whole thing amusing!

I knew that in about a quarter of a mile, this path would open onto a much wider path that had been used to clear wood with oxen…and that led directly home. In other words, a ten minute walk at the most. Because the boulder lay directly in the curve, the path continued on parallel to us about six feet below. The problem was that the path was so narrow that Shadow would have to place his hooves *in front of each other* – and the edge of the path dropped off steeply into the chasm.

I decided to go ahead and climb down to a section where only grass grew, while Shadow stood above me and waited for a signal. I had knotted the reins together, so that I had an almost 12 foot long line. Thank God that Shadow had learned to move one leg at a time in our trail exercises! No one can tell me now that Western riding is good for nothing!

I directed him step-by-step and inch-by-inch down the slope until he was safely down and next to me. I was so relieved, but I couldn't fully relax until the narrow path finally opened onto the wood-clearing path.

When I think about how nervous – even hysterical – Shadow used to be, I'm all the more proud of him. When it was most important, I knew I could rely on him 100%. After this little adventure, we spent two more wonderful weeks at the ox stable before we made the trip back to our own stables.

Shadow gets mobile

While Shadow and I were up at the ox stable, my dad found a classified ad for an inexpensive secondhand horse trailer – a "one and a halfer," which is designed for transporting a mare and her foal.

We drove up to look at it anyway.
The trailer was as old as I am and didn't look that great – although with a splash of paint and some elbow grease, we could make it look nice and be fit enough for driving!

Now I finally had my own trailer for getting to the shows. This was a giant step forward!

Since the trailer was a little too wide to just put Shadow in and too narrow to build a divider, we took two big sheets of foam rubber, covered them in cloth, and upholstered both inside walls of the trailer. Shadow quickly saw how comfortable it was for him if he leaned against one of the foam walls when we were driving.

We fixed up the entire trailer, inside and outside. We painted, put in a new floor panel and a new top. It looks a little odd, but I'll never give it up because Shadow loves it. He actually enjoys riding in a trailer because he has so much room and a window to look out of.

Roundup Festival in Obersoulzbach, 2001

Shortly after we got back to our home stable, I got an unexpected phone call. Dieter had the habit of calling up out of the blue – and he usually had fantastic ideas when he did!

He told me about a little Western festival that was coming up in France, about 60 miles away. He was in the process of coordinating the annual show he stages there…and said he would love it if Shadow and I joined him.

I knew it would be fun to do something like this with the folks from Red Rock, so I agreed to come. Of course, I had no idea what I was getting myself into!

Dieter came over to pick up Shadow and then we drove together to Obersoulzbach. I took one look at the set-up – and the huge riding arena (nearly 90 yards long and 40 yards wide) and suddenly realized this would be more than just a small town fair.

The next day the festival got under way – and I was totally bowled over. Where did all these people come from? Later I found out that more than 5,000 people had come for the show. Great, I thought. Our first out of town show and it has to be in front of a huge audience. A few of the performers were even famous, like Jean Marc Imbert, who is world-renowned for his liberty horse dressage and stunt numbers.

And little Shadow and I were supposed to perform here?

"Just keep it simple and it'll all work out," said Dieter as he pushed me into the riding arena. It's a strange feeling when suddenly 5,000 pair of eyes – sparkling with anticipation! – are fixed on you.

At first I was afraid that the loudspeakers and hordes of people would make Shadow nervous and forget all our cues – but boy, was I wrong!

Instead, the exact opposite happened – all the attention from the crowd seemed to transform him. He raised his head, held his muscles taut and, with his eyes blazing he seemed to say, "Look at me, I am the greatest!"

He mastered his first big show perfectly. Everything worked on the first try. When he went to lie down, I was suddenly the one who was nervous. The ground was still wet from the nightly rain, except for a small area where they put down sawdust. Would Shadow be willing to lie down here? In front of all these people?

I gave him the cue and Shadow sank down with his usual serenity, first to his knees and then all the way down. The audience burst into applause and Shadow twitched. At first I thought that he would jump right back up again. I wouldn't have blamed him, because the applause was so enthusiastic that it almost broke my concentration too!

But Shadow was curious and just turned his ears in all directions before lowering his head again to play dead. He turned his head to me as if to say, "What's going on? Don't you want to play pillow again?"

Naturally I sat right down with him and he put his head in my lap and lay quietly while Dieter, with his stallion, "Hollywood's Lead Man," rode a reining around us. The crowd cheered and clapped for Dieter's fast maneuvers, but all Shadow did was twitch his ears periodically. He didn't try to get up at all.

Until I cued him to getting into a sitting position. He sat up straight as an arrow and began to wave with his front leg. The audience loved it and gave us a rousing round of applause as we left the arena.

Who would have thought that deep inside of Shadow was a real show horse, just waiting to come out? He seemed to shed all his fears – in fact he seemed to truly enjoy all the commotion!

Obersoulzbach would not be the only show we performed in that year. We started off small and if it weren't for Dieter's contacts, we would never have gotten off to such a good start. He took us to three more shows that summer: at a small riding club near his ranch, at a dog club, and to a genuine Indian Powwow. We made a few bloopers along the way until we had our routine down pat, but Shadow always played along obediently.

Red Rock Show Day, 2001

In September, Dieter hosted another open house at Red Rock Ranch – and he was expecting Shadow and me to perform again. We practiced a little freestyle number, which worked well at home. Shadow quickly learned to chase after me and play "catch," and had a lot of fun doing it. Sometimes he had too much fun and got so carried away that I had to slow him down a bit or he would have run me over in his excitement!

For our second number, I wanted to ride Shadow using only the neck ring – no saddle or bridle. We had to do a lot more practicing to get that down, but Shadow decided he didn't like this trick and didn't want to practice at all. He made his displeasure abundantly clear; when I tried to practice the Spanish trot, he'd only go backwards in protest. After a while he stood with his backside to the fence and refused to budge in either direction. He got a little slap from me for that, which made him so angry that he reared up suddenly. He took me so completely by surprise that I couldn't get out of the way in time.

Shadow's big head knocked into the bridge of my nose. I heard it crack and then everything went black for a second. When I refocused my eyes, I blinked and saw blood running down Shadow's shoulder. My blood.

My nose was bloody, my vision blurry and I felt queasy. The farm owner took me straight to the emergency room and the others brought Shadow to his stall. I had a nasty concussion, a hairline fracture of my cheekbone and I wasn't allowed to ride for the next few days. When we did start practicing again, Shadow seemed deeply remorseful for what he did. He was on his best behavior and we had our number down perfect.

Sadly, we had no luck with the weather that year. In the week leading up to the show, torrential rains turned the riding arena into a swamp. Nevertheless, because so many people had come out to see the performances, we decided to go through with the show, regardless of the weather.

Shadow had improved considerably over the past year. In our freestyle number, he walked away from me twice to inspect the riding area with his head held high, but when I called him he returned to my side immediately. The riding number came off perfectly and both performances were a big hit with the audience. No doubt we'd return again next year!

Shadow and the All-round Course, 2001

After a while, Shadow got bored with just shows and circus training, and I had to come up with a new idea to challenge the little fellow. When Agnes Henet, a well-known trainer, offered another trail course, Karen and I signed up with Caven and Shadow.

Agnes and I had known each other for a long time, and she was thrilled to see how much Shadow had improved. Although he still had a tendency to be nervous and inattentive, he tried hard to master even the most difficult trail exercises. We learned a lot in those lessons. More importantly, I discovered that Shadow had a real talent for trail and I started thinking about training him for a tournament next year.

Meeting Sita

It was a very cold day that second Sunday in December when I took Shadow to a small nearby riding club to participate in a Christmas show. It was our first performance in an indoor riding hall. But it wasn't going well. Shadow didn't feel comfortable in the narrow stall there, and during training he was so tense and nervous that as we left the hall, he accidentally stepped on my foot and broke my little toe. Wonderful, I thought. Now I have to participate in a three-hour show with a broken toe. At least I had the right shoes on already. If I had had to change them first, then my toe would have swollen up even more.

Shadow didn't like the riding hall, and during the freestyle number he tried to find a way out. His concentration was off completely. When our part of the show was over, I brought Shadow to his stall and took care of him before returning to watch the rest of the show.

I got back just in time to see Sita Stepper and her stallion, Doc Smokey Dry. She rode a complete trail without saddle or bridle and then did reining. The whole thing looked so harmonious that the audience was literally speechless. I was thrilled watching her, and thought that if all western riders handled their horses so sensitively, then the sport would have a decidedly different reputation in Germany.

After the show I rushed over to her and thrust my business card in her hand. I told her that I would like to photograph her horse some time.

At the time I would never have believed that one day, Shadow and I would be with her at Mocha Oak Ranch!

Shadow gets sick

Shadow didn't have a very good winter. Shortly after the Christmas show he started to cough. Every day it got worse and worse. I didn't know what was wrong and asked the veterinarian to stop by. He concluded that Shadow must have had a herpes infection as a foal, which so weakened his immune system that it never completely recovered. We had no choice but to give Shadow very strong medicine to treat the cough and then hope for the best.

The farmer offered to move Shadow to a different stall where he could soak his hay for him.

But Shadow didn't feel comfortable in the new stall without his paddock and – literally – climbed the walls. After two weeks we had no choice but to move him back to his old stall.

We drove to a special feed dealer 120 miles away to buy some special alfalfa feed. It meant a lot more work for me because the grains had to be soaked, but at least Shadow's cough improved.

Our first tournaments, Summer 2002

By springtime, Shadow's health had improved greatly. The alfalfa helped him put on some weight and he was slowly starting to look quite handsome.

My friend, Eva, decided she wanted to start in some amateur tournaments this year with her Thoroughbred, Apollo. And I decided Shadow and I would accompany her, to see if they were something for us, too.

Our first tournament was an amateur-riding tournament in Ichenheim. It was a catastrophe. Shadow was so nervous that all he could do was prance from side to side. He barely managed to clear any of the obstacles. The announcer's barbed commentary didn't make it any easier on us. It was all I could do to keep Shadow under control during the endurance competition – and even then he almost bolted.

After this first, disastrous tournament I seriously considered canceling our appearance at the Mocha Oak Ranch tournament in a few weeks. Shadow didn't seem to enjoy performing any more and I didn't want to force him to participate. I had managed to build up

his confidence quite a bit during the winter, and I didn't want to ruin that with wrong-headed ambition.

On the other hand, I didn't want to throw in the towel after one bad experience, so we drove off to the Mocha Oak Ranch after all. From the start, Shadow seemed to feel at ease there and he was much calmer during this tournament. He even took third place in Horsemanship and Pleasure!

With new motivation, we headed off to the Western tournament in Ichenheim – and believe it or not, Shadow was successful here as well. He took fifth place in Trail and sixth in Pleasure. I was more than satisfied with our performance. Our last tournaments of the year were the amateur endurance competition in Ottenheim and Kehl-Sundheim. Once again, Shadow scored in the upper half – and we both had a lot of fun! He seemed to slowly understand that tournaments aren't something unpleasant to be feared…and as a result, he started to truly enjoy himself!

Since things were going so well with the Western tournaments, I decided that Shadow and I would accompany Eva and Apollo to a few dressage tournaments as well. We didn't have a dressage saddle, but Eva lent us her show jumping saddle. She also gave me a performance outfit. After a few weeks of practice, we started in our first dressage tournament class E in Ulm, a small village in the Black Forest.

It was a minor catastrophe. It was our first tournament and Shadow had to ride at the very front. The horse behind us galloped too close behind and then started to shy wildly, totally confusing Shadow. In other words, our first dressage tournament was not exactly a smashing success.

But that didn't matter to me. A few weeks later, we started at a tournament in a senior citizens' facility. Shadow and I had given a small performance there the year before. He was familiar with the set-up and the people were very nice to us.

Eva and I washed our horses' manes the evening before the tournament and then braided them. To keep the horses from getting dirty, we covered them in lightweight summer blankets and told the farmer that under no circumstances should they be allowed onto the pasture the next morning.

Guess where we found our thoroughly dirty horses the next morning? Of course; on the pasture. The farmer had let them out a half hour before we arrived and smirked maliciously as he watched us frantically trying to clean them up.

Somehow, we managed to get to the tournament on time. While the organizers of the tournament were very nice, the other riders made fun of Shadow because he was so much smaller than the other horses. They laughed that his coat was a "strange" color and his saddle so old and unfashionable.

But when it was Shadow's turn and they saw how obediently he completed his test, and his lively stride and elegant manner, the unkind commentary stopped. Clearly, they were impressed with the "little circus horse."

Everyone except the judge, that is. He gave Shadow exceedingly low marks. Spectators, as well as other riders, just shook their heads – no one had expected such poor marks.

Afterwards, a rider in Class A dressage came over to me and said, "Don't take it too seriously. That judge can't stand small horses and he likes white ones least of all. He always gives warmbloods the highest marks because they have the better gait."

Nevertheless, Shadow had improved considerably since the last tournament – and that was what mattered most to me. Still, I decided to focus more on Western riding in the future.

Round Up festival in Obersoultzbach and smaller shows

Dieter rang me up again in June to ask if Shadow and I would like to come along to Obersoultzbach. Of course we would! This time around, Shadow would be performing two show acts – a circus number on the ground and then a riding number with the neck ring, together with Dieter and Sunflower. He was very well behaved and went along with everything. He seemed to enjoy the applause more and more!

We attended a lot of smaller tournaments and shows during the summer of 2002 as well. Shadow and I got some very valuable experience that would most certainly help us in the bigger shows we'd be competing in next year. We also had a whole lot of fun. The only downside was when some clubs tried to worm out of paying the appearance fees we had agreed upon. By the end of the summer, I had concluded that I wouldn't accept every offer to perform. After all, transportation and preparation for a performance cost a lot of money. If we weren't paid for our performances, then I was out a hefty sum – money I'd rather spend on more important things like high quality fodder or Shadow's training – in the long run, that would be much more beneficial to him!

Shadow moves in at Mocha Oak Ranch

I had been having problems at the stable, and I finally realized it was time to leave. But where could I get a new stall quickly?

Our first step was to move out to the ox stable to put a little distance between some unpleasant episodes with the farmer and us. The quiet did Shadow a world of good and I didn't have to worry about him. That gave me a little time to look for a new stable. Unfortunately, there

wasn't anything suitable in the area and Shadow and I couldn't stay at the ox stable forever. One thing was for sure – I definitely didn't want to go back to the farmer.

So one day, I visited the Mocha Oak Ranch and asked Sita if she had any room for Shadow. Fifteen miles was a long drive to get there, but it was the only one in the entire area that appealed to me.

I lucked out! A stall with paddock would free up in the fall – and Shadow could have it.

The Mocha Oak team took good care of him from day one. At first Shadow was allowed out on the pasture alone. Then other horses were allowed out one by one to see which ones he got along with. After a two-week adjustment phase, Shadow was allowed on the pasture with a big herd of horses. At the beginning he liked to pick fights with Trott, the lead horse, a commanding Merens gelding. But Trott quickly put the impertinent new fellow in his place and showed him who was boss around here.

In less than four weeks, Shadow was a new horse. His constant unease seemed to dissipate day by day. He began eating huge amounts of hay and you could almost watch his weight – and muscles – grow.

He felt at home here and I knew that I had made the right decision.

Red Rock Show Day, September 2002

Originally we had planned to move to Mocha Oak after Dieter's open house. But our sudden change of plans turned my schedule upside down. All the moving-related chores had left me with hardly any time to practice the show numbers with Shadow.

Still, despite all the stress both of us suffered this summer, Shadow gave a masterly performance at Red Rock Ranch. He thrilled the audience with a circus act and riding without a headpiece.

Dieter was especially pleased to hear that Mocha Oak was Shadow's new home.

Winter at the Mocha Oak Ranch – new friends

Mocha Oak had a really good riding arena for training, and for the first time ever I realized what a powerful gait Shadow had! He seemed to float over the ground!

Here, nobody gave us funny looks or laughed at us for our circus exercises – on the contrary, people seemed to be genuinely interested. One day Sita came to me and asked, out of the blue, if I could possibly show her how to do it, too.

She wanted to do something a little different than "just" riding with her stallion, Smoke.

Smoke was the first stallion that I did circus exercises with, and I was delighted with the speed at which this impressive quarter horse learned – and how enthusiastic he was about it. I had to be careful not to make Shadow jealous, though, so Sita began riding him while I worked on circus exercises with Smoke. Sita is a terrific Western trainer and rider, and although Shadow didn't know how to do very much when he was saddled, she was thrilled by how hard he tried to do everything right.

Three other people who used to keep their horses at the other farmstead moved over to the Mocha Oak that winter. They had come to visit Shadow and me and wound up liking it so much that they also decided to move here.

Sabine's son, Alexander, and Chris's son, Sascha, suddenly decided that they wanted to learn to ride here. But they were a little afraid of the other horses and only wanted to ride Shadow. That's how Shadow got a new job that winter as a children's school horse for the two boys. All three of them had a lot of fun!

Shadow and the composure test, January 2003

Shortly before Christmas, Dieter called. He was interested in offering something new, the so-called "composure test." He asked if I could write about it in my capacity as a journalist.

But frankly, I was more interested in participating with Shadow than writing about it! Since the test required a good deal of practice, I decided to take Shadow over to Dieter's ranch a week early. We wanted to practice mastering the different obstacles with the other participants every evening.

In the composure test, the horse is led past different "fright obstacles" and the judges evaluate the horse's ability to stay calm. The horse has to pass by a running tractor, pull a noisy sack, cope with balls being rolled in front of him and much more.

At first Shadow didn't like these exercises at all and started to fool around. My first thought was that we'd never manage. But when it was our turn to take the test, he really pulled himself together. Out of a possible 10 points, we received 9.8! I was so proud of him and how he was finally facing his fears and not running away from them.

Shadow gets sick again!

Spring came and the preparations for the Mocha Oak Ranch tournament were going full speed ahead. I was practicing a few show acts with Shadow when I noticed a small open wound on his jaw. I figured it was a bite or a big wasp sting – and did nothing.

The next day the inflammation covered Shadow's entire face! His hair was falling out, his skin was hot and pus oozed all over.

I called the veterinarian immediately and he diagnosed a severe fungal infection. While it wasn't life threatening, there was no guarantee that his coat would grow back in time for the tournament in two weeks. Shadow needed several kinds of medicine, salves, and a special cleansing lotion, which I had to use twice a day to clean the infected area. He wasn't allowed to go out to the pasture with the other horses because the fungus was extremely contagious. He had to stay in his stall for two weeks, more or less alone, and he didn't like that one bit. After a week, he looked much better, and I didn't give up hope that all would be well in time for the Ranch festival.

Shadow at the Mocha Oak Show Day, May 2003

The atmosphere was nice at the Mocha Oak Ranch Show and Shadow had fun performing. He gave a marvelous performance and Alexander and Sascha helped out. He also mastered his first act with the long reins wonderfully. Eva participated in another show number with Cindy, her German Shepherd-Husky mix, who at this point can do as many tricks as Shadow. The tournament was a great success for Shadow – he placed in every discipline that he started in!

Tournaments, Summer 2003

Over the course of the summer, we started in a few genuine Western tournaments and Shadow almost always placed. It was quite challenging for him because he was starting against expensive quarter horses that have been trained by professionals. Still, he always gave his all and made a good impression.

We went back to the ox stable again this summer – this time Karen and Caven joined us. Caven and Shadow had a lot of fun together and romped about the paddock and around the house like two wild yearlings. They were so crazy that our houseguests often just shook their heads in disbelief. At the ox stable we also started shooting the first photos for a book about circus exercises that I'm currently working on.

Seven at once!

While we were out at the ox stable, I discovered by coincidence that Shadow had a talent for several tolt variations. His gait grew faster every day we spent riding in the mountains until one day it was practically a racing gait! Since I used to work a lot with gaited horses and even wrote a book about this type of horse, I had enough basic knowledge to get a horse into a tolt – but I had never actually *done* it myself!

Fortunately, though, Shadow and I had become an excellent team over the past few years, and I knew him well enough to anticipate how he would react to certain cues.

Saddled up and with the snaffle didn't work at all, so I laid a thin Navajo blanket on his back, secured it with a girth and bridled him with a hackamore. Then we rode uphill and downhill – and as we went downhill, Shadow soon fell into a tolt-like gait!

It didn't take long before I had trained Shadow in three different variations that I could cue specifically: one is the so-called Spanish Walk, which has *nothing* to do with the circus exercise, Spanish Trot. This gait got its name from the horses the Spanish settlers brought to America. These horses commanded a very fast gait – think of it as "power walking" for horses. The second variation was the Fox Walk, a kind of tolt with a diagonal gait. It's what the Missouri Foxtrotters are known for. And the third gait is a specialty of the Tiger Horses, known as the "Indian Shuffle." For this tolt variation, the horse raises his legs on the diagonal, like he would in a trot, but he lowers the back leg a little faster than the front leg. It looks a lot like a trot, but is much more comfortable for the rider.

Soon Shadow had mastered eight different gaits:

1. The standard Walk
2. The standard Trot
3. The standard Gallop
4. The Western Jog
5. The Canter, a four-beat gallop
6. The Spanish Walk
7. The Fox Walk
8. The Indian Shuffle

At the moment, we're working on other gaits, such as the Running Walk of the Tennessee Walkers and, of course, the Piaffe, the Passage, the Redoppo and Mezair. I think it'll take another four years at the most before Shadow becomes the first 10-gaiter in the world!

Red Rock Show Day 2003

The Open House show at the Red Rock Ranch was almost a complete washout. On Saturday, the weather was okay, but when I finished my Midnight Show, the first big raindrops started to fall. On Sunday, it poured in buckets. All day long. But the spectators came anyway. Armed with umbrellas and raincoats, they stood shivering around the riding arena.

So we performed our entire act and, although Shadow doesn't like being out in the rain, he pulled himself together and we managed both shows without any major problems. After us, Sita went on with her new fire act. Dieter was grateful that the two of us came, even though we had the longest distance to travel. A lot of other performers didn't even bother to show up because of the bad weather.

A relaxing winter, 2003

Our second winter at the Mocha Oak was quiet and uneventful – which was exactly what Shadow needed. It was a very cold winter, however, and we decided to keep Shadow in one of the stalls overnight to prevent his cough from coming back. Every morning he came over to the big sandy arena for his morning exercises. He had time to run around for two or three hours, while Eva fed and cared for the other horses. I usually trained with him around midday. We fed him a small portion of warm mash or linseeds almost every day, to be sure that he put on a little weight. Then he was allowed out to the winter pasture with the other horses to frolic together for a few hours until twilight. It was a very restful winter for Shadow.

We worked hard on improving his skills with the long lead and we also spent time in the round pen. I rode Shadow three or four times a week, but I rarely used the saddle most of that winter; just the side pull. While it was bitter cold, it was also very dry and we had lots of sunshine – Shadow and I soaked up energy for the coming year.

High quality Tiger!

Thanks to my work as an equine journalist, I have a few contacts to breeders and breeding associations in the US. One day, while working on something else, I came across the homepage of the Tiger Horse Registry in New Mexico, an organization I had worked with years ago on a book. I decided to get in touch again, and sent along a photo of Shadow, to show them what my horse looks like.

The next day, I received a reply and after a few pleasantries, the head of the Registry wrote that Shadow looks just like a Tiger Horse…and that she'd like to see a few more pictures and a video as well. Maybe she could issue him papers!

I put together a collection of photos right away and then asked Gabor, Sita's husband, to film Shadow's gaits. I was excited at the thought of Shadow's genetic ancestry finally being deciphered, because so far, no one had been able to tell me what kind of a horse Shadow is!

I quickly sent everything off to New Mexico. A few weeks went by without any news and I figured oh well, that was that, and assumed they weren't interested anymore. But then an email arrived. They wrote to say that they had examined all the information I had sent them, and that they would like to include Shadow in the Tiger Horse Registry!

I couldn't believe my eyes! At the moment, not even 100 Tiger Horses are registered around the world because this association has such high standards – and suddenly, Shadow has the opportunity to be included in this handpicked group of horses that had originally been bred for princes!

The Tiger Horse has its origins in the border area between China and Siberia and used to be called the "Heavenly" horse. Kings and princes of China and the Asian steppe used these colorful horses with the special tolt gaits to hunt tigers – which is where the name "Tiger Pinto" came from.

But this breed more or less died out more than 1000 years ago. In America, special breeders are trying to bring it back. And since the Registry is first and foremost interested in quality, not quantity, they have very high standards for potential members. Shadow more than fulfilled their standards and was registered as a "High Quality Tiger." As such, he is the only recognized Tiger Horse in Europe, because right after his registration, the breed book was closed. Now the only horses that can be registered as Tiger Horses are those whose parents are already registered!

The adoptive daddy

Shadow's and my single life came to an end in February 2004, when Ingo came into our lives. He had never really had much to do with animals, so he was extremely skeptical that he and Shadow would get along – especially since Shadow gets jealous easily.

But they both got on marvelously from the moment they met! Ingo liked Shadow so much that he wanted to get in on the action and tried his hand at ground work in the round pen. Shadow turned the tables on him and directed Ingo more than the other way around. But both had a lot of fun doing it. One day, Ingo just swung himself up on Shadow's bare back and rode off with him as if it were the most natural thing in the world to ride around the ranch without a saddle or a bridle. Everyone there was amazed. Ingo was so excited that he decided to really learn how to ride and to come along to Shadow's shows and tournaments.

Shadow never really had a buddy among the other horses, but Ingo seemed to fill this role perfectly for him. It wasn't long before they were best friends.

The horse musical

Once again I got an unexpected phone call from Dieter, who had an offer for a new show. An acquaintance of his was holding a Western tournament near the Swiss border. The highlight of the evening was to be a horse musical. He wanted Shadow and me to play a role within the framework of the musical, and we were supposed to give a twenty-minute performance!

Of course I agreed and, on April 23rd, we drove off to Schlingen, near Basel. The weather was mixed and it looked like the event might be called off because of rain. Because it was Shadow's first performance after the winter break, he was almost overeager and had nothing but foolishness in his head.

Bernhard Prokop organized the tournament. He's an Appaloosa expert, and has even judged Western tournaments in the US. From the start, he was enchanted by Shadow's charm. Then Shadow performed the "Shadowy Hide" act in "Lord of the Rings." It wasn't an action-packed number or one with a lot of special effects – I wore a long white dress and rode Shadow with a cord around his neck through several dressage moves, all to the music from "Lord of the Dance." But the audience loved it.

Shadow participated in the tournament as well – I thought it would be a good start for the season. His head was full of foolishness

again and he didn't perform up to his normal standards, but it was enough to place in Trail, Horsemanship, Pleasure, Reining and Freestyle Reining. I had had a complete Bedouin saddle and bridle custom-made in Egypt for him over the winter, and it looked great on him. I decided then that this outfit would be one of our top show costumes – after all, you need to give the audience something new every year!

Mocha Oak Ranch 10-year anniversary, May 2004

We wanted our Mocha Oak Festival to be something really special that year; after all, we were celebrating our tenth anniversary. So Sita and I sat down together to think about what else we could do in addition to the usual tournament disciplines and performances. We came up with the idea of including a Freestyle Reining, a Halter class, and an evening show on Saturday night. That meant twice as much stress for us, but we wanted something memorable.

Shadow and I started in a higher class in all disciplines that season: Showmanship at halter, Trail, Horsemanship, Pleasure, Reining and Freestyle Reining. Once again, Shadow gave a solid performance. In Showmanship, he took second place and in Freestyle, our "Bedouin Fantasia" took first place! We also placed well in all other disciplines.

On Saturday and Sunday, we staged a colorful show as well. On Saturday, Shadow took the spotlight in the riding arena as "Shadowy Hide" from the *Lord of the Rings* and seemed to literally enchant the audience.

We needed two days to recover from the stress of this weekend, but it was a complete success!

Sweet itch

The summer of 2003 was hot, but the summer of 2004 seemed to drown in rain. Sometimes I asked myself if we had just skipped over the summer and gone straight to autumn!

Since it was hot in addition to being damp, we wound up having a lot of mosquitoes – millions of them, and they seemed to drive our horses out in the pasture simply insane.

One day, Shadow started scratching his tail. He rubbed his backside so hard against the iron rod of his paddock that he turned black from it. At first we didn't think much of it. I washed Shadow and he got a worm treatment. But the problem didn't stop. Soon he started doing the same with his mane.

I was a little unsettled and called in the veterinarian. He diagnosed a very mild form of summer eczema.

This news hit me hard. I feared that this might spell the end of Shadow's show career. It didn't matter much to me if he scratched off some of his mane and tail hair – but who wants to see that in a show? And really, it's not too pleasant for him, either.

Thank heavens it wasn't a full-blown case yet and we were able to get it under control with a special diet, cleansing lotion, and skin oil. That kept it from developing into a big problem and we were able to go on tour again.

Roundup Festival in Obersoultzbach, 2004

Last year we hadn't been invited to the Obersoultzbach festival because the event manager supposedly found someone whose horse was even better at circus tricks than Shadow. But this year we were invited back.

We had a beautiful deep blue sky on the Saturday that we traveled there. On Sunday, two hours before the show was to start, the weather turned and we had pouring rain and lightning! All of us sat together with Dieter in his RV and hoped that it would clear up soon.

Either way we'd be doing our show, but we couldn't film or photograph the performances in the rain.

Amazingly, about twenty minutes before we were supposed to go on, the storm front passed and the first rays of sun shone down. By the time it was Shadow's turn, the sky was almost completely blue again! As always, we performed two show acts. The first was circus exercises and the second was an Indian riding number with neither saddle nor bridle that we performed with Dieter.

After the show, Noel came over to talk to us. Noel lives in Alsatia and is the Chief of the "Plains Indians," in addition to performing with the stunt-riding group, "Crazy Riders." He asked if Shadow and I were free in two weeks to come to an event he was hosting about six miles from Obersoultzbach. It was a genuine Indian Powwow with dancers, singers and over 50 teepees!

Shadow and the jumper riders, August 2004

Exactly one week after that Western tournament, Shadow and I were scheduled to give four big performances at the gala evening of a jumping show at the same location. I drove there with mixed feelings. In the past, I'd had bad experiences with English riders and was more than doubtful.

But the people there turned out to be incredibly nice. We were allowed to park our trailer on a meadow right next to the arena, and Shadow had the whole meadow to himself. At night, they even provided him with a stall, in with the extremely expensive tournament horses.

The riders were also very friendly. They were astonished when Ingo, in a fit of boredom, jumped onto Shadow's bare back and played ball with him on the meadow, without a saddle or bridle.

The evening's show was Shadow's longest performance ever – four show numbers at ten minutes a piece. First the long rein and circus exercises, followed by a western riding number, then our Bedouin Fantasia and finally, "Shadowy Hide" from *Lord of the Rings*. Shadow had never appeared in such a large arena – 75 by 75 yards! That was twice as large as the riding arena at home – and sometimes even that one made him uneasy. But the audience enjoyed our show and we were paid the fee that we had agreed upon. All in all, my opinion of jumper shows improved dramatically! Indeed, there are nice people and not so nice people here and in every other kind of riding sport. At the small tournament last year I had less luck with the people, but here I met nothing but nice folks.

Shadow at the Plains Indians Powwow, Steinbourg, August 2004

The next morning, we drove with Shadow to France for the " Powwow." We arrived to see a sprawling teepee city. The program had a lot to offer. Noel was a generous host to Shadow, Ingo and myself. He showered us with meal and drink tickets and Shadow got a shady paddock.

Shadow was all wound up the night before and had a lot of foolishness in his head. During our riding number with the neckring, he Piaffed the whole time – although he hadn't yet learned

the Piaffe! But the audience loved it. They were thrilled by the "white stallion." *Stallion*? Well, he certainly acted like one!

After my show, a member of the famous stunt-riding group, the Crazy Riders, came over to us and asked if she and her horses could try out Shadow's ball. Of course, no problem! It makes me glad when we're able to inspire people to try out new things. Noel was so impressed with Shadow that he wanted to come to the Mocha Oak with his stunt horse during the winter to learn circus exercises from us!

Our first reference book!

After two years of work, the time had finally come in August – our first reference book was published. It was entitled, "*Harmony Between Horse And Person – New Methods For A Trusting Partnership*." In my book, I describe Shadow's journey, and how he went from being a troubled horse to a celebrated show star thanks to our circus exercises.

The book was released just before the Americana, in which Shadow was to be introduced to a wider public.

Shadow in the press

It's a crazy thing: you work really hard for years and years and nothing happens. Then – bang! –everything happens at once.

I got an email from the Tiger Registry, telling me they would like to forward a few photos of Shadow to "The Gaited Horse" magazine in the US. I agreed, but didn't hear anything more for a while – until the day I received a small package from the US – and in it was an article about Shadow in "The Gaited Horse!" In a four-page story, the Registry discussed Shadow's history – and how proud they were to be able to include him in their register!

We hadn't yet been at the Americana, nor had my book come out – yet reporters were already lining up to talk to us. Countless newspapers wrote stories about Shadow. The German magazine, "Pferde Heute" ("Horses Today") ran a feature article on the Tiger Horse breed that included pictures almost exclusively of Shadow. Other magazines also showed intense interest in him.

I could hardly wait to see what would come next! But I had to start concentrating on the Americana. That was the most important event of the year for us, and it could even launch a bigger career for Shadow…

Shadow at the Americana, 2004

The Americana is the biggest Western riding event outside the US. It takes place every two years and is *the* highlight for every European Western rider. I had contacted the Americana back in October 2003, just wanting to introduce Shadow to them. I never dreamed that they would actually invite us! But the Americana committee likes to give newcomers a chance, and so Shadow and I got 45 minutes in the "Forum" on four of the five days of the event. In the Forum, we were flanked by some of the most famous Western riders and horse whisperers in the world! I got butterflies in my stomach when I read a copy of the schedule and saw who would be in the Forum besides us – almost all of my greatest role models! I started to feel pretty insecure and wasn't sure if Shadow and I were up to this challenge. Unfortunately, we had to do without Ingo on the first day, because he had to work. So I took along Sabrina and her boyfriend, Andy. Sabrina and I had gone to a lot of amateur tournaments together and I knew I could count on her.

Sita and Gabor also came along with Smoke. Sita had hesitated for quite some time before deciding to register her horse for these European championships. Although Smoke was the German champion in Superhorse last year, the Americana was another class altogether, in terms of competition. But we finally convinced her and so, on September 4th, we drove off to Augsburg with two trailers and an RV. September 8th would be Shadow's first day in the Forum with me because that was the official first day of the fair, but I thought it would be better for him to arrive a little early to have time to calm down and get acclimated – plus we could watch Sita prepare for the competition and wish her luck.

The first day, I went into the practice hall and lunged him. He was very excitable and everything seemed to frighten him. He kept coming over to me and trying to hide behind me! It wasn't until the second day that he became more confident, and then I took him into the big arena. Two years ago, I had come here for the first time as a journalist. At the time I thought that if only I could come here with Shadow – that would be a dream come true! And now, just two years later, here we were, in the big arena, surrounded by Europe's best Western riders!

Smoke performed magnificently in two advance rounds and made it to four finals: Superhorse, Western Riding and two Pleasure categories. That was more than all of us had expected! And then he pulled off the highlight of the show! With an incredible score of 148.5, Shadow's nine-year-old stable buddy trumped

the international competition to take the title "World Open Champion Superhorse." That's the highest award you can get!

In other words, Smoke stormed to the pinnacle! Now it was our turn to do our best in the Forum.

A German Western retail catalog outfitted Smoke and Sita and Shadow and me for the Americana – really chic clothing and accessories, which helped Shadow and me look a whole lot more "professional."

But could we meet the high expectations everyone had for us?

The first Forum was on Wednesday, September 8th. I was extremely nervous and excited. Although I had lunged Shadow in the smaller Forum ring for the past few days, it's still something completely different when there are a lot of spectators around.

Even though it was a Wednesday, every space around the ring was taken, and all the spectators stared at us, full of anticipation. Shadow and I were the first show in the Forum, and a lot depended on the first impression that we made.

Shadow was wonderful – even though he wasn't used to staying intensely concentrated for 45 whole minutes! The Forum director was more than satisfied with his "new discovery," and was tremendously encouraging to us.

The other Forum participants didn't look at Shadow suspiciously or pejoratively – on the contrary, most found him to be delightful, which motivated us to persevere.

On Thursday, Shadow was much calmer and more motivated – maybe because Ingo made it just in time for our appearance. Both of us were happy that he had finally made it. The greatest problem in the Forum was performing the tricks in exactly the same sequence. Because Shadow had such a good memory in this respect, he sometimes did his own improvisations while I explained to the audience what we had just done. And that truly wowed the audience because they could see that Shadow genuinely enjoyed what he was doing!

On Friday we had the day off, which did Shadow a world of good because the performances were quite strenuous for him. Every day, Sabrina rode a little with him in the riding arena – and wherever Shadow went, it wasn't long before he drew an audience that wanted to watch him goofing around.

On Saturday, we had an appointment with the official photographer of the fair. I felt Shadow deserved to be photographed in front of the big Americana screen, just like all the other tournament horses.

To get there, we had to walk clear to the other end of the hall, past all the breeders and their information stands in order to reach the photographers' stand. When we got there another horse was still being photographed and we had to wait a while.

Shadow wasn't the least bit nervous. He stood there and observed the colorful goings-on with great interest. And before we knew what was happening, he started snacking on the pretzels that had been set out for guests at the neighboring stand and pulling the hats off the heads of passersby.

Then it was finally our turn, and Shadow was allowed to stand in front of the big photo screen. Suddenly a crowd of people gathered to watch. Shadow felt so important! When he was supposed to rear up, he catapulted himself straight up and whirled his front hooves in the air. The photographer was so astonished that he almost forgot to snap the picture! He was used to tournament horses, which prefer to keep all four hooves on the ground. When Shadow did it again, he was ready and took a great photo.

Right after our photo session, two ladies from the Italian Chamber of Commerce appeared. I recognized them from horse fairs that I had attended in the past. We had discussed the possibility of Shadow performing in Italy at the Fiera Cavalli some day. As long as both they and Shadow were here, I figured I might as well give them a taste of what he could do. We had a little time before our next turn in the Forum, so we went over to the practice area. They took a lot of photos of Shadow and seemed to be really excited about him. In their opinion, Shadow could become a big star in Italy, too.

I had no time to think about what they had said, because we were due in the Forum.

On Thursday, I thought things were pretty crazy at the Forum. But today – it was incredible. Every seat was taken. And people *stood* four rows' deep in back, just to get a look at what was going on in the Forum ring!

Shadow seemed to get a little stage fright because he kept trying to hide behind me. But on second thought, he probably did that because a band was playing very loudly next to the ring and one of the exhibitors was demonstrating his pasture fences, which made loud cracking noises. Shadow was quite nervous, but once again he pulled himself together and reliably demonstrated each of the exercises. Even lying down was no problem, although with all the noise and all the people, I would've understood if he had refused. Afterwards, people streamed to our stand and we sold a lot of books. I was so proud of Shadow, but I was also glad that tomorrow would be the last day of the Forum. We were all exhausted.

On Sunday, Shadow, Ingo and I were left to our own devices because everyone else had gone home already. And although all my helpers were gone, this turned out to be the most quiet and stress-free day of all. We took our time getting Shadow ready and then walked over to our last Forum appearance. There was no loud music or cracking noises today, so Shadow was the picture of calm and seemed to savor his last appearance.

Everything worked out perfectly and the Forum announcer said later that Shadow made a tremendous impression on all the spectators – and that he planned to recommend us for the Americana 2006!

When I brought Shadow back to his stall, tears started to stream down my face. Only now that it was over did I understand what had happened here.

My little Shadow, my ugly duckling, the horse I bought five years ago because nobody else wanted him.

My little Shadow, who once hated people and almost landed in the slaughterhouse.

My little Shadow, the horse people used to mock and laugh at, saying he would never amount to anything…

My little Shadow was now a star.

He appeared at the Americana. Countless photographers shot pictures of him – and once we got home, the requests from magazines that wanted to write about him were rolling in. Even *television* had been in touch: they wanted to film a piece about "Shadow – the heavenly horse" with us at the Mocha Oak Ranch! Thousands of people watched our Forum appearance and laughed, smiled and applauded.

Shadow made it. The dark chapter of his past was sealed forever and a new life could begin .

But that is another story.